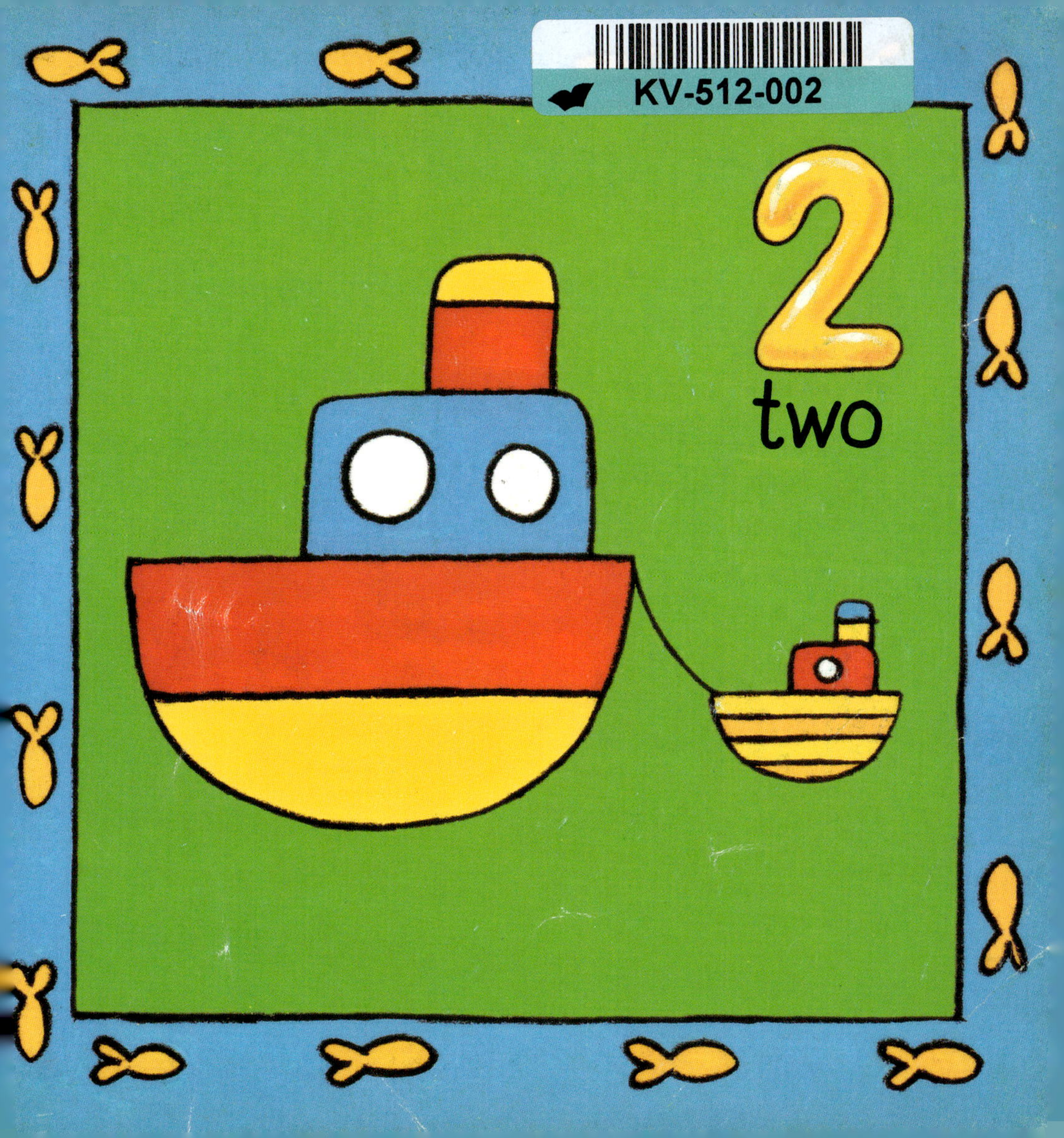
2
two

3

three

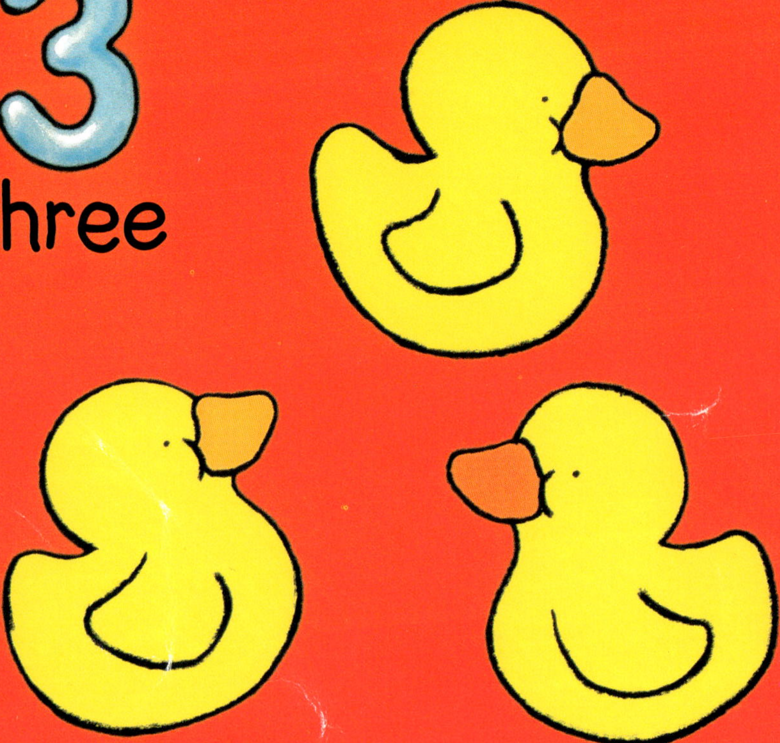

4

four

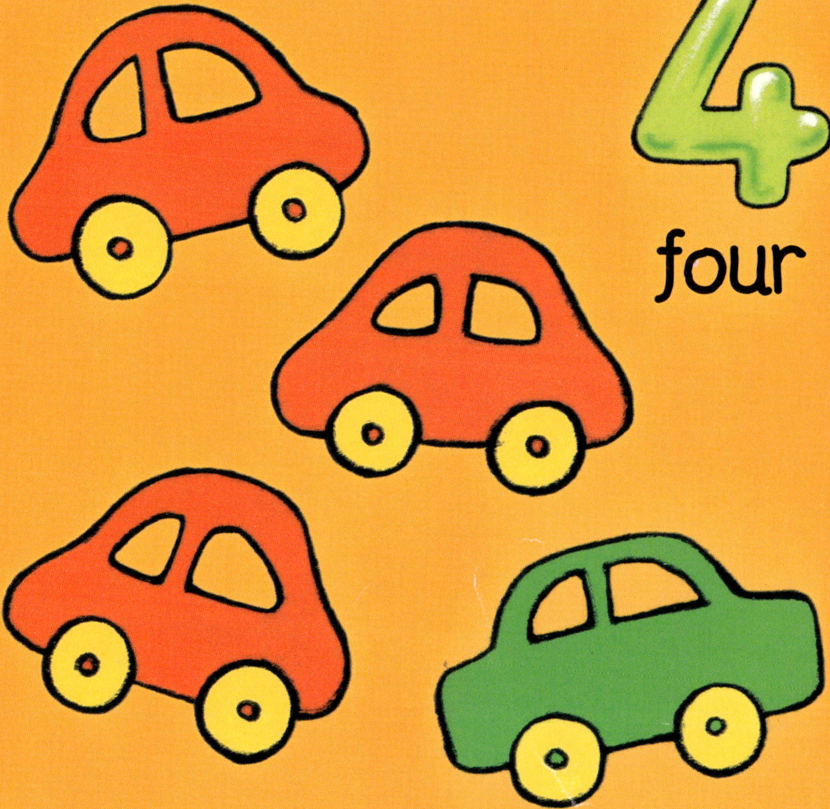

5

five

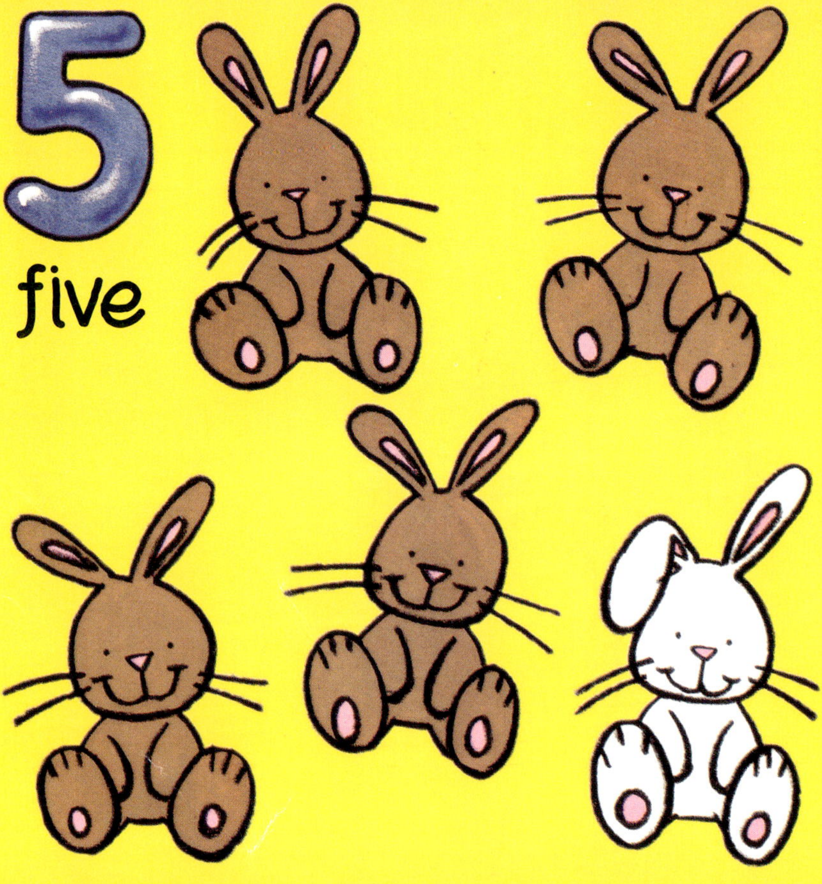

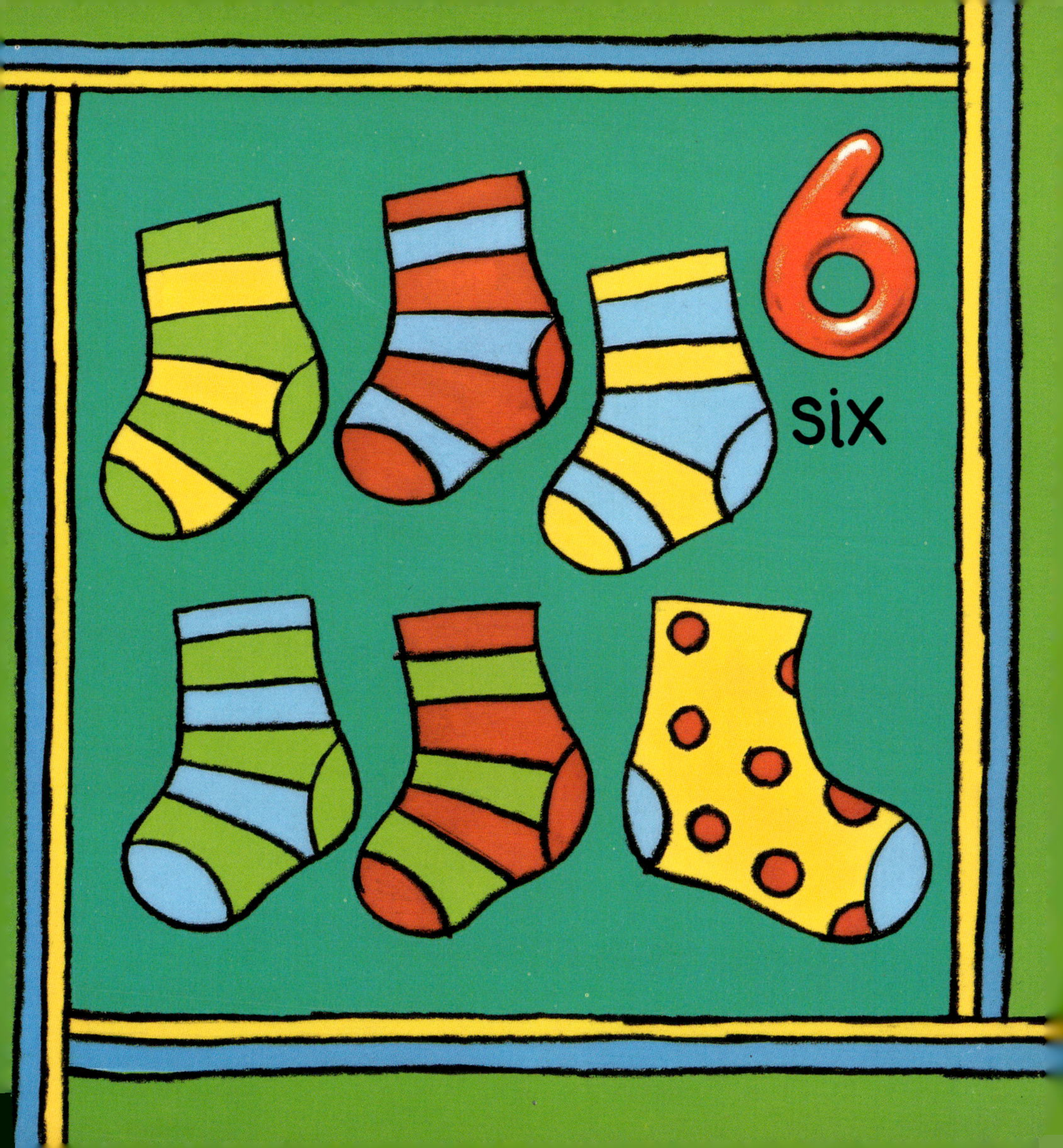
6
six

7

seven

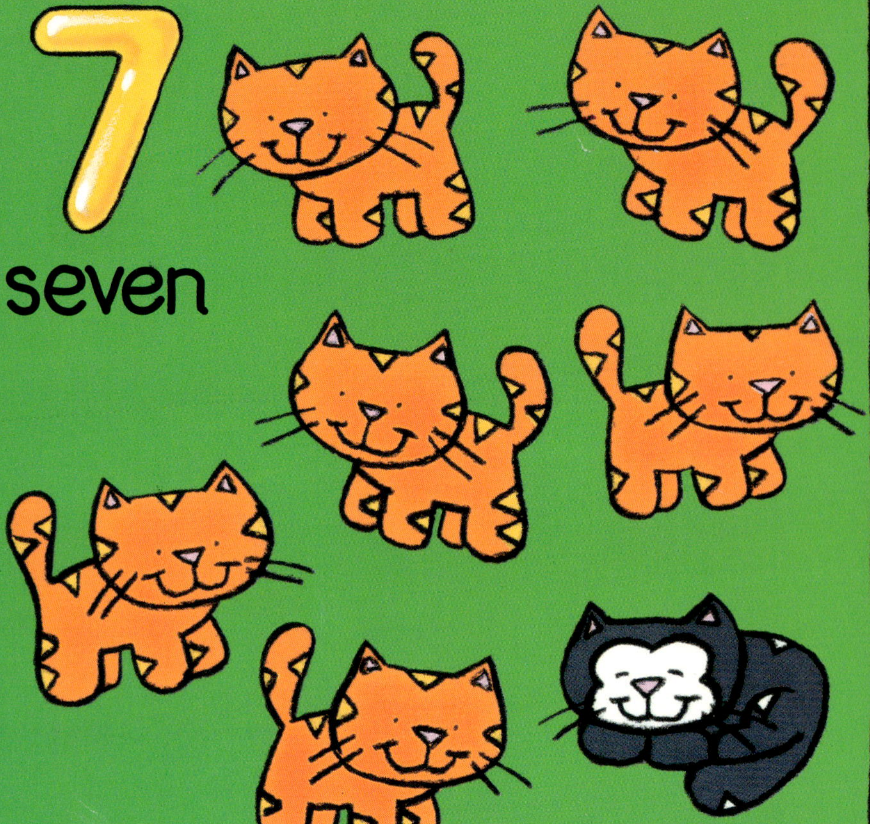

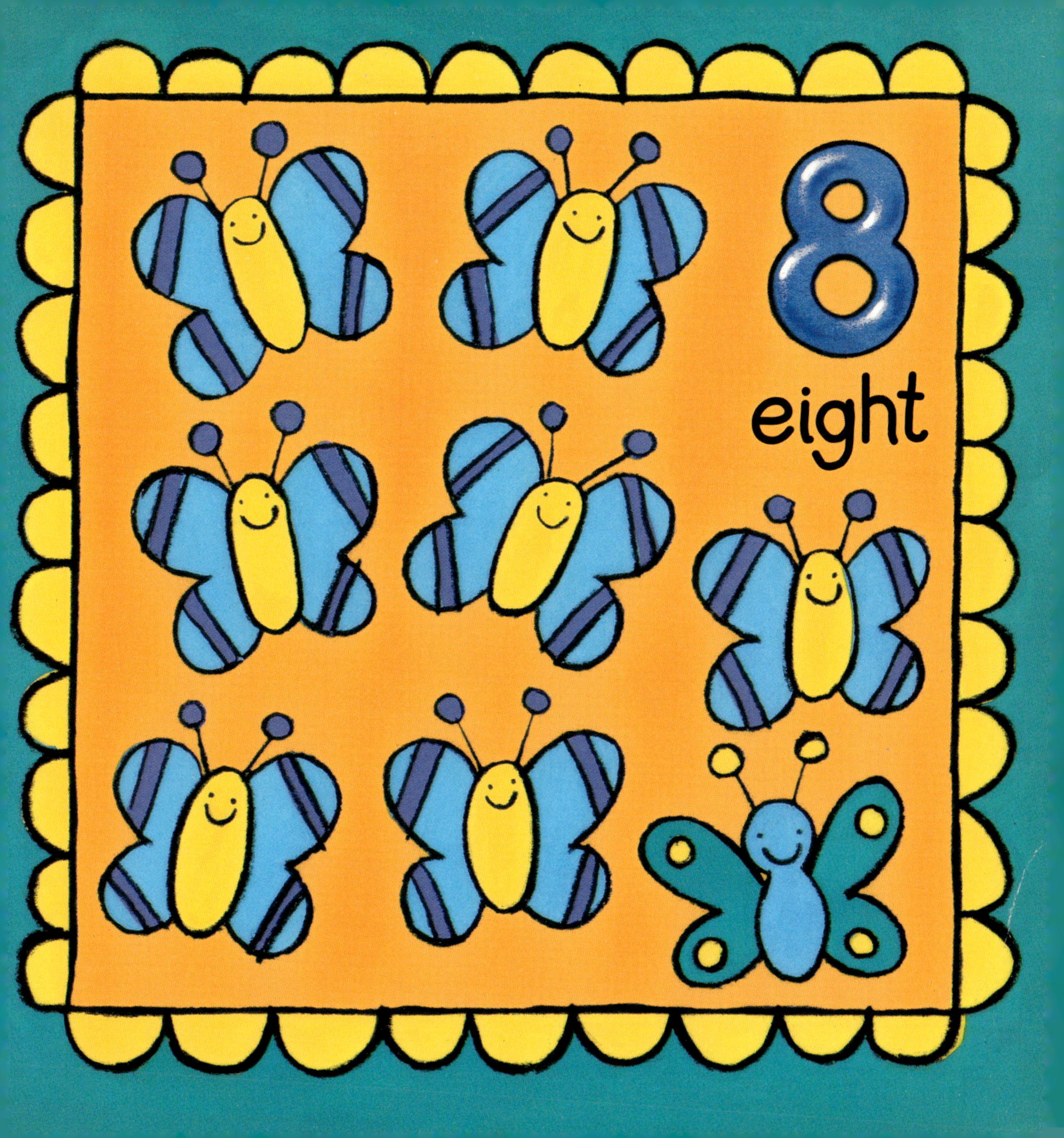
8
eight

9
nine

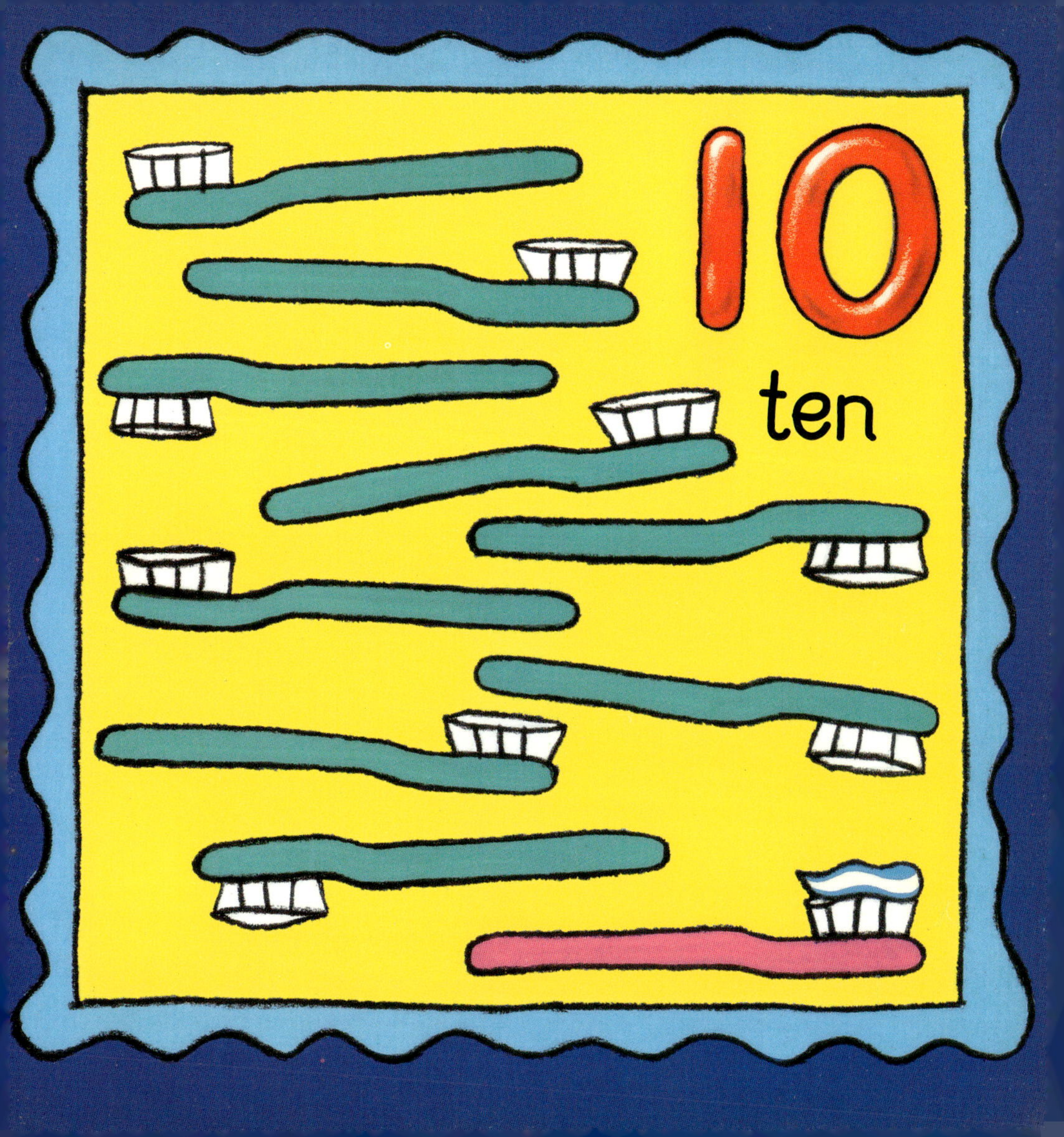
10
ten

11

eleven

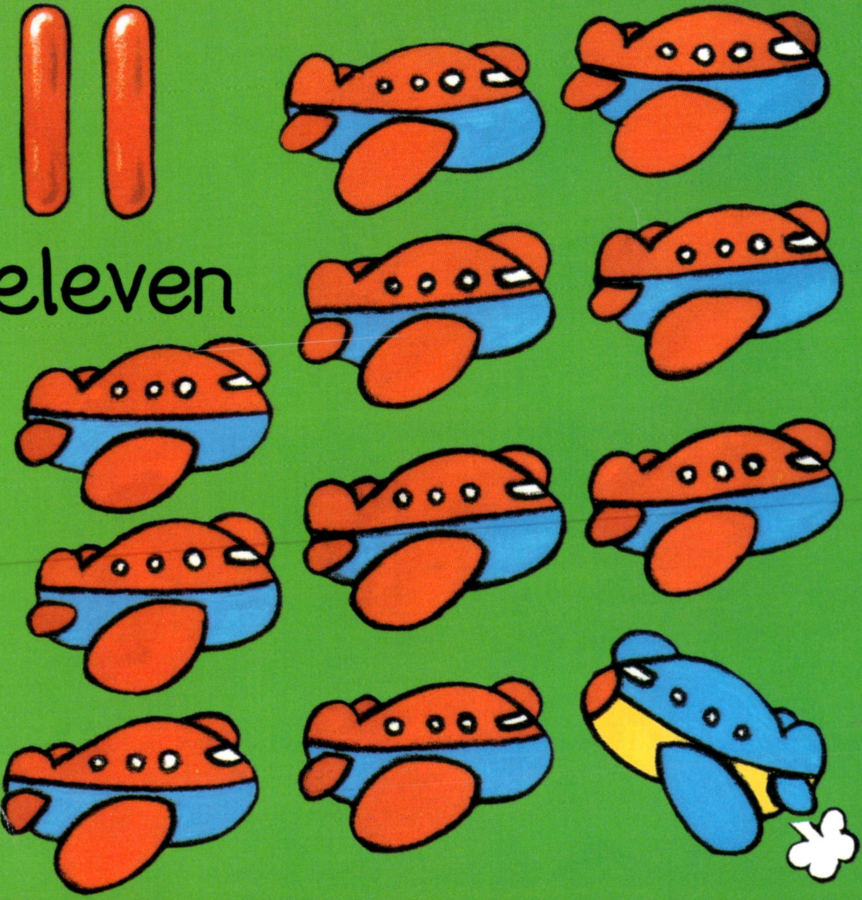

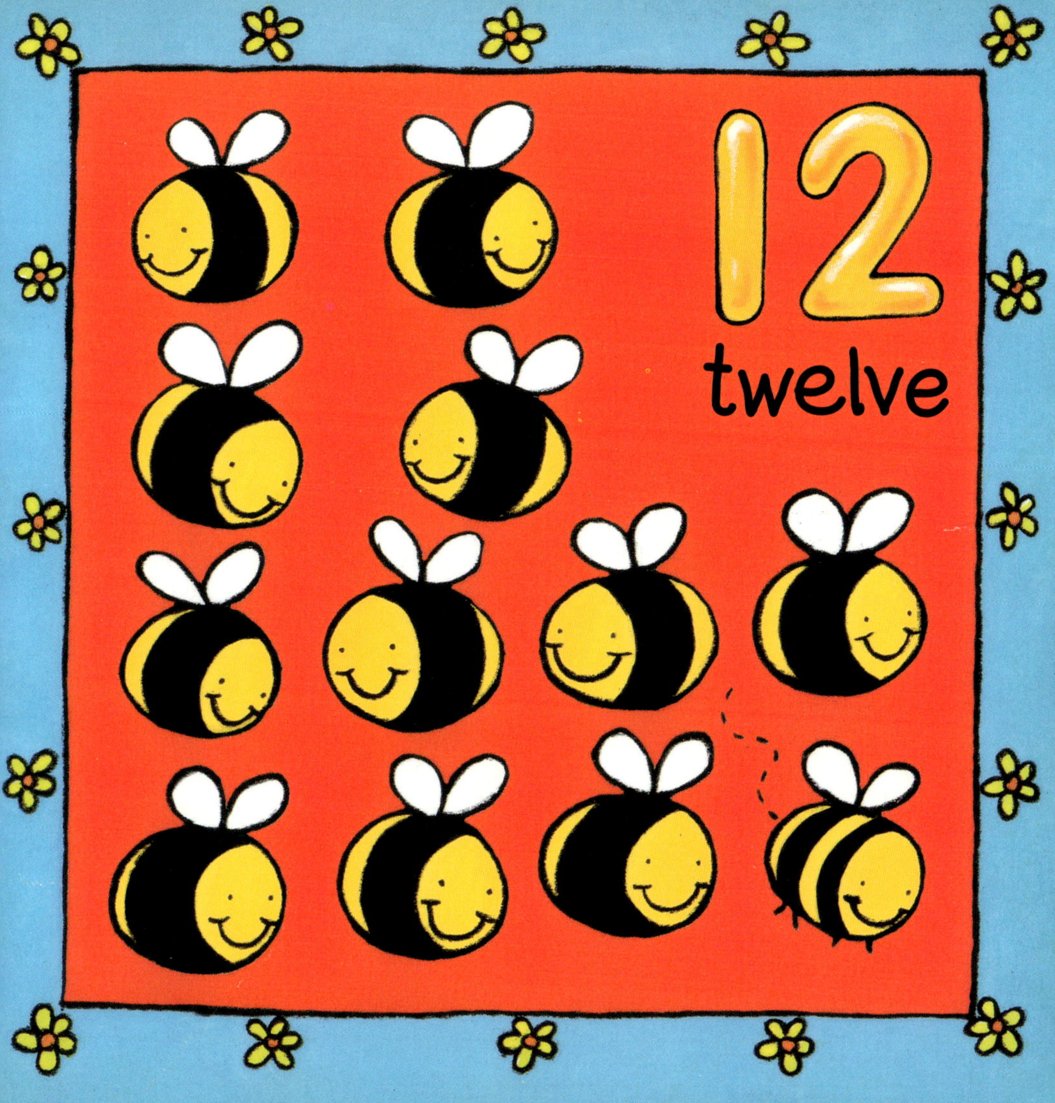
12
twelve

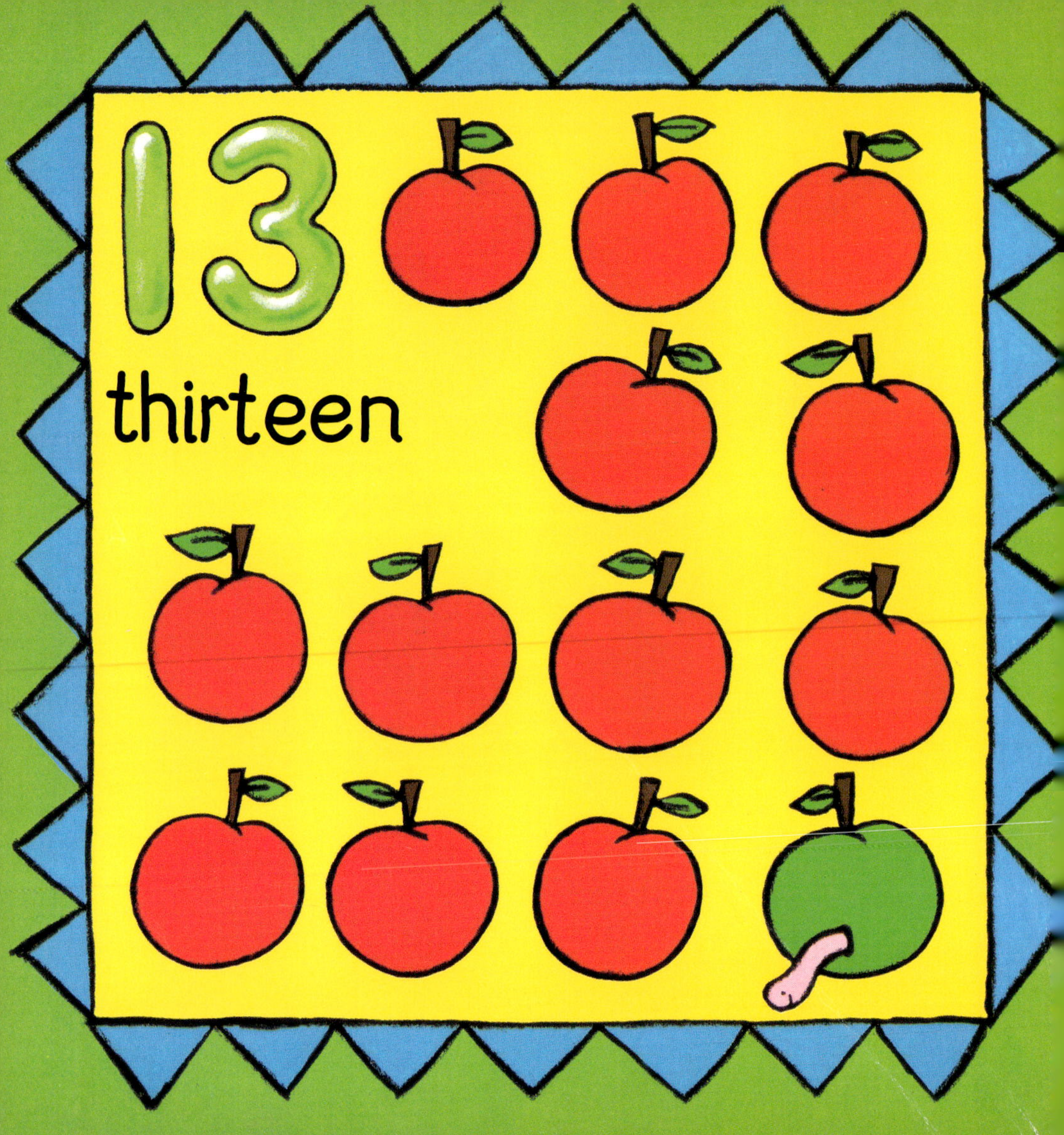
13
thirteen

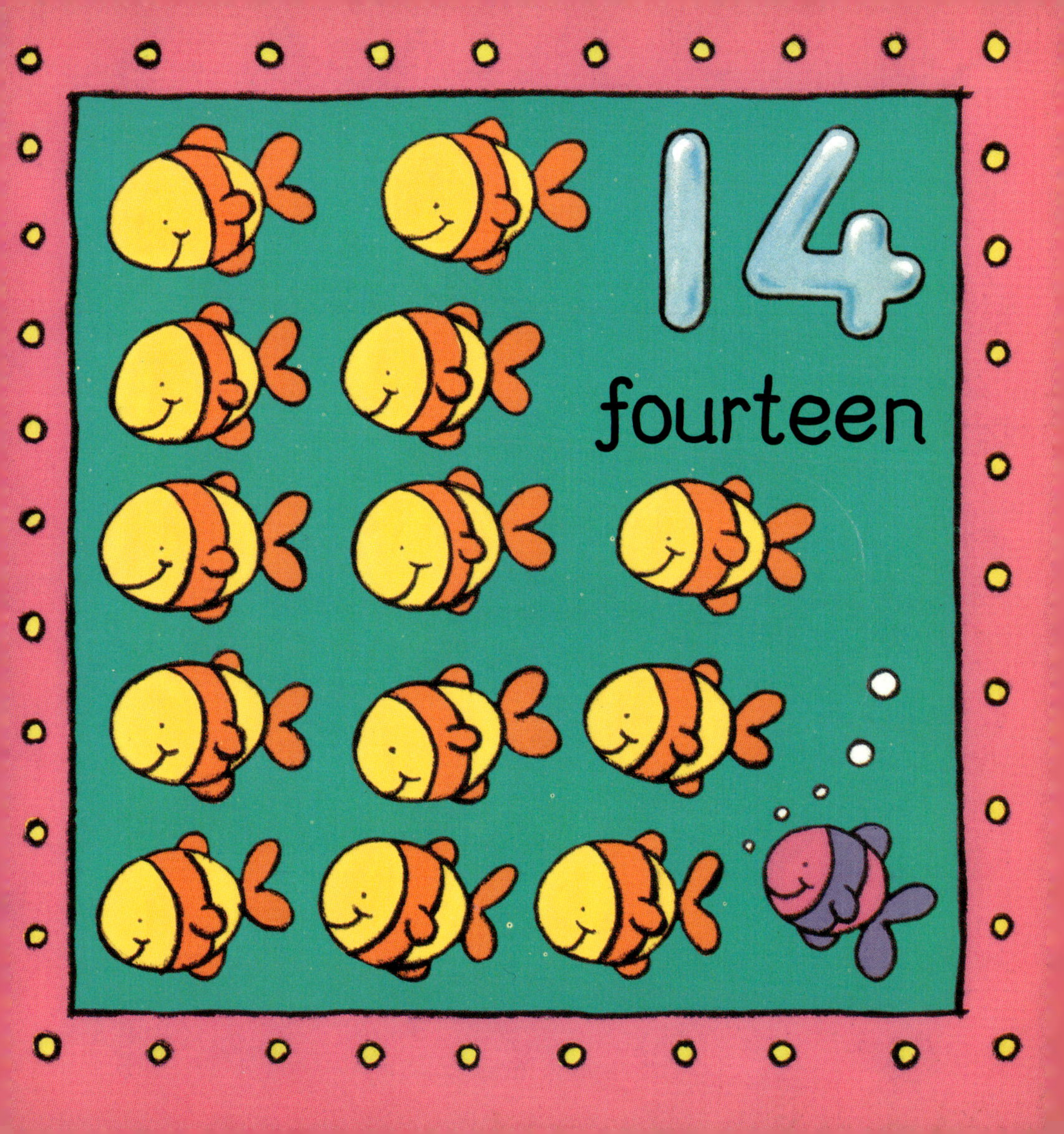
14
fourteen

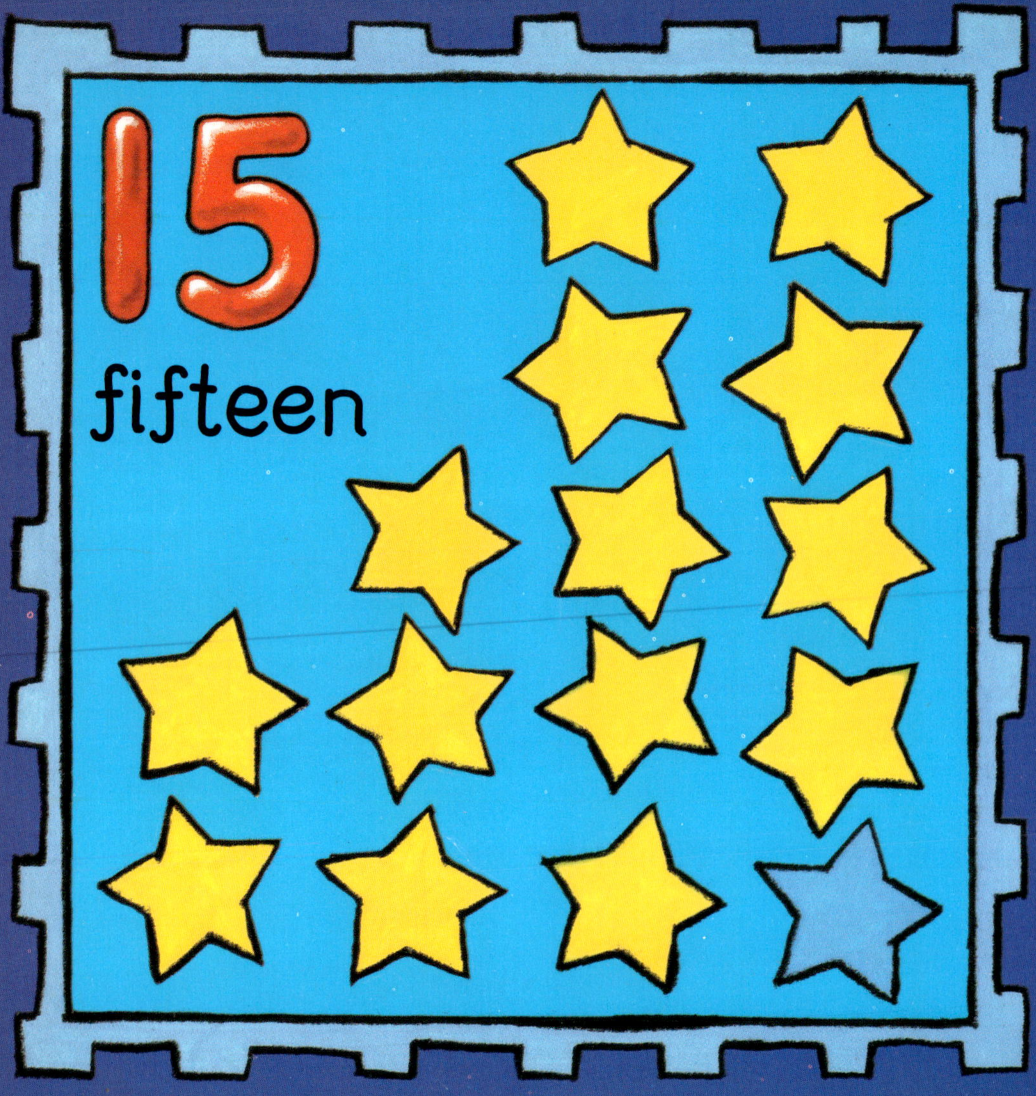
15
fifteen

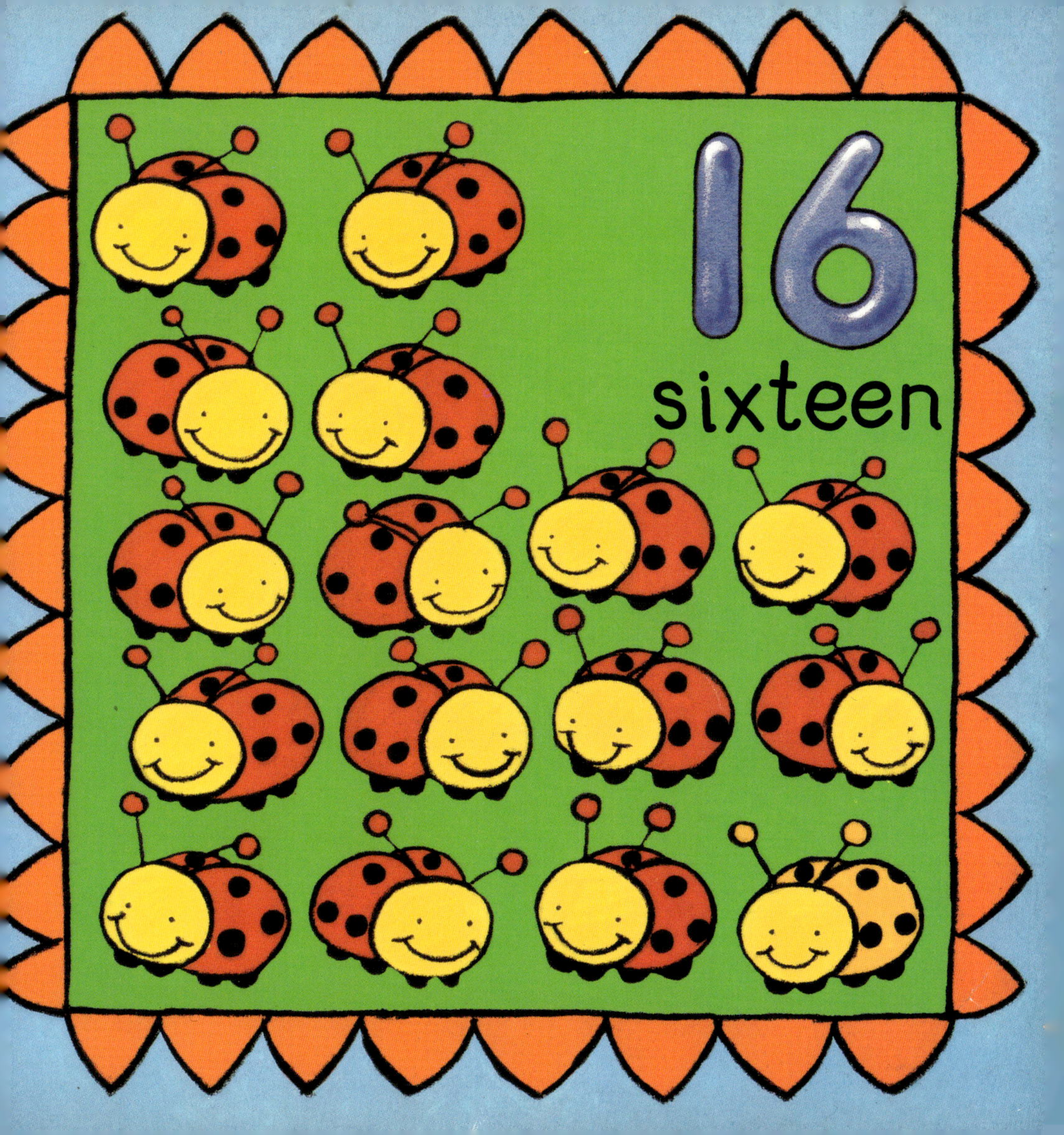

16

sixteen

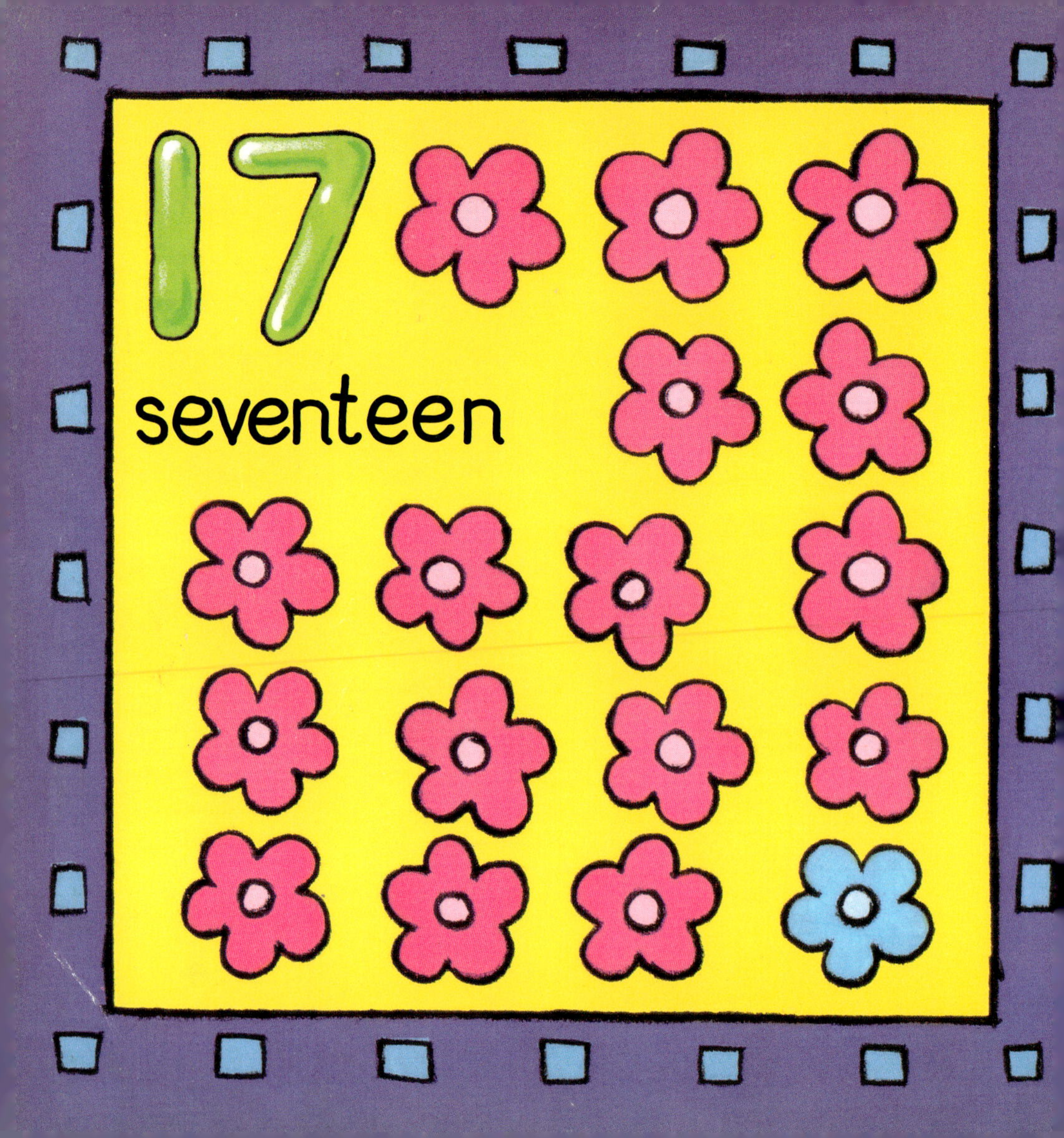
17
seventeen

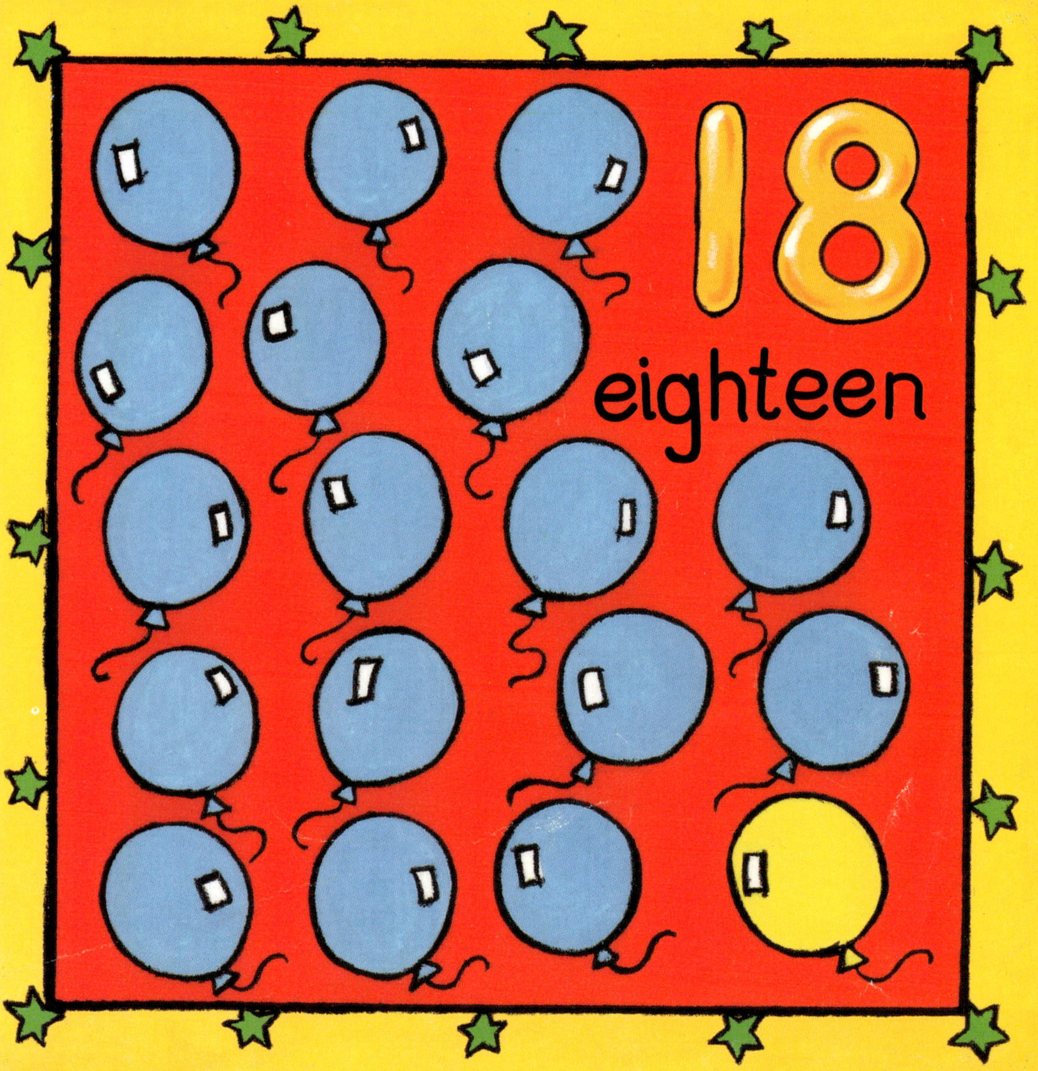
18
eighteen

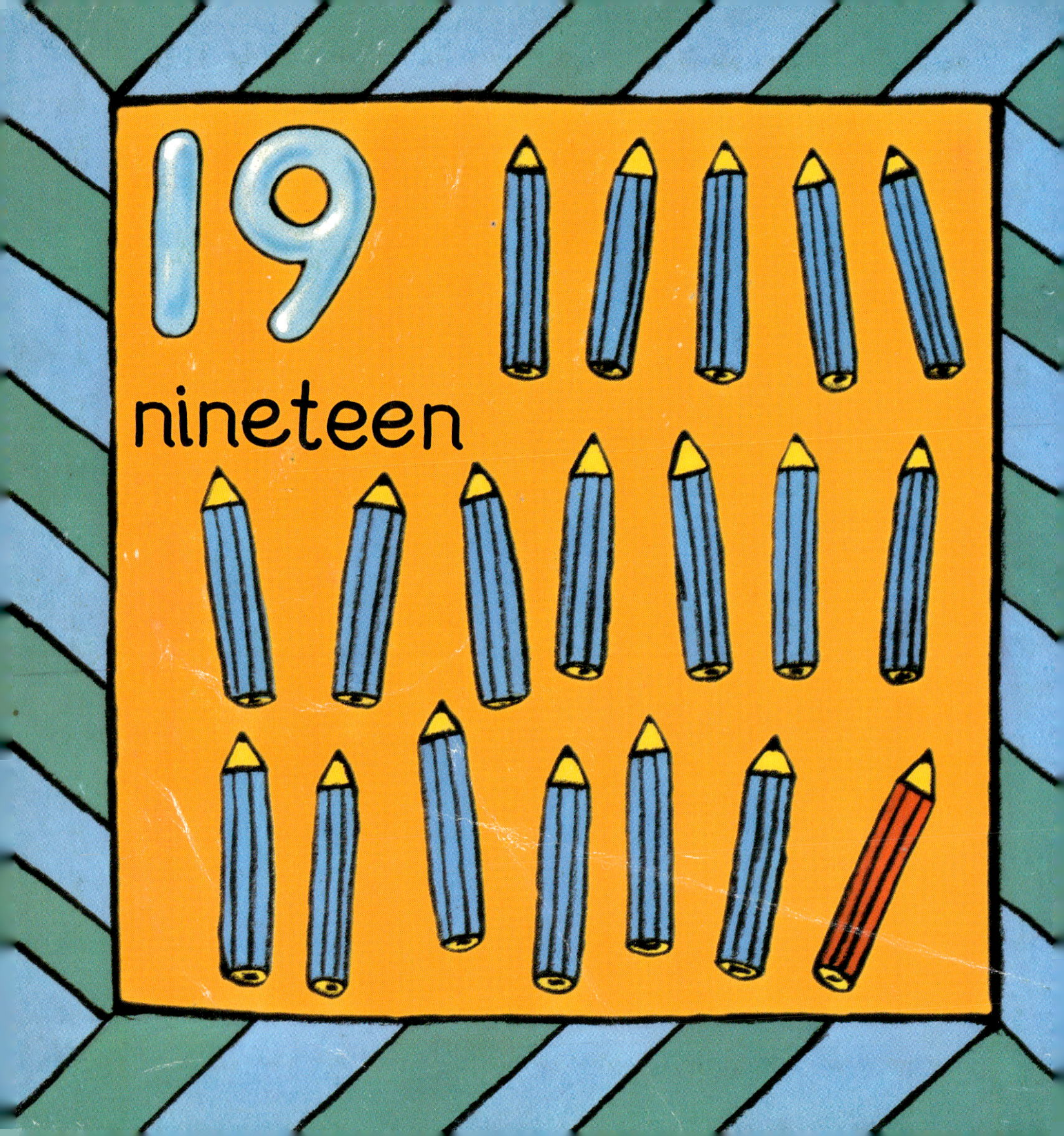
19
nineteen